Flying High

Flying High

Sara Grant

Illustrated by Erica-Jane Waters

Orion
Children's Books

First published in Great Britain in 2013
by Orion Children's Books
a division of the Orion Publishing Group Ltd
Orion House
5 Upper St Martin's Lane
London WC2H 9EA
An Hachette UK company

1 3 5 7 9 10 8 6 4 2

ISBN 978 1 4440 0779 4

Printed in Great Britain by Clays Ltd, St Ives plc

To Montana Edwards and Brittany Murray –
cousins and best friends – wishing you many
magical adventures together

Chapter One

Trix leaned forwards and aimed her broom for the stars. She shot off like a rocket, bursting through a thick, fluffy mattress of clouds. Speeding through the clouds felt like being tickled by a thousand feathers. The wind whipped through her curly brown hair as she flew higher and higher and faster and faster until Little Witching was a twinkly blur below her.

Flying was the best feeling in the world.

At least she hoped it would be . . .

. . . when she learned how to do it.

Trix opened her eyes.

It was only a daydream. Her trainers – one black and one white – were firmly planted on the floor of the magic classroom hidden in the Little Witching Primary School library. Her dream of flying seemed as far away as Little Witching was from the dazzling rings of Saturn.

"My little witches, before we can fly we must create our vehicles!" Lulu exclaimed.

She waved her broom in the air and set her bracelets jingle-jangling. Lulu was their magical teacher from the Sisterhood of Magic. It was her job to teach Trix and the four other new witches – Stella, Pippa, Cara and Becka – the art of magic. The girls looked like proper witches with the tiny pointed hats Lulu had given them – but they had a lot to learn. The best and brightest witches would become fairy godmothers one day.

Was it only last week that Trix had turned ten and discovered she had the gift of magic? Trix still couldn't believe she was a witch with her own magical familiar – a black and white kitten named Jinx who was only visible to witches. She had to keep her new magical powers and her amazing invisible kitten a secret from everyone – even her best friend Holly.

"Witches fly on besoms," Lulu explained. She held the broom straight out in front of her. "A besom is a very special kind of broom. Like your magical rhyming spells, your besom will be unique to you. Once each of you has created your very own besom, we can start flying lessons."

Trix's tummy got all fluttery with the thought of actually flying. She studied Lulu's besom. It had silver and gold bands spaced up and down the broom handle, matching Lulu's bracelet-filled wrists.

"Um, what's it called again?" Pippa asked. Her high blonde ponytail flipped from side to side as she looked from Lulu to the sticks in the centre of the room that they would use to construct their brooms.

Stella laughed, but it wasn't the nice kind of laugh that friends share. Stella's laugh was forced and seemed to be thrown like a ball of stinky cheese. "It's called a besom, silly."

Pippa blushed. Her familiar, a lavender rat named Twitch, climbed out of the pink handbag that was slung over Pippa's shoulder. Twitch scampered up Pippa's arm and curled around her neck. "Thanks, Twitch," Pippa

whispered and brushed her
cheek on the rat's soft
lavender fur.

Trix knew how Pippa
felt because Stella usually
saved all her meanness for
Trix. Stella, Cara and Pippa
attended the Enchanted
Grove School for Girls,
and they *usually* stuck
together.

"We do not call other
people names, Stella," Lulu said and
made Stella's name sound like a bad word.
"Neither Pippa nor her question is silly.
Questions are rainbows to knowledge." Lulu
clapped her hands and returned to her witchy
lesson. "There is no right or wrong way to
create your besom. The only thing it has to
do is fly. Now, let's get to work!"

Trix let her hand hover over the pile of
long, thick branches that Lulu had supplied
for the handle part of the broom. Her fingers
tingled as she came to a crooked branch with

bumps all over it. "This is it," she whispered to Jinx. She picked it up and noticed that the lines in the bark seemed to swirl.

Jinx helped Trix line up a bundle of sticks at one end of the handle. Trix carefully wove the twine in and out of the branches. Jinx batted at the ball of twine, chasing after it when it rolled away. As Trix worked, she noticed the twine change from a dull brown to a shimmering rainbow of colours. She must be doing something right!

"Finished!" Stella said and raised her perfect broom over her head. Trix noticed that she'd turned it nail-polish pink. "That was easy peasy! I'm ready to fly."

"We will fly when *everyone* has finished their besoms," Lulu said. "This is not a test of speed but of creativity." As Lulu inspected the other witches' brooms, Trix took a sneaky peek too. Cara and Becka were nearly finished. Their besoms looked like proper brooms – except the twine on Becka's broom was plaited like her own brown hair, and the end of Cara's broom was twice as bushy as everyone else's.

"Look at Pippa's!" Stella pointed and laughed. It seemed to Trix that Becka and Cara echoed Stella's laugh even before they'd looked in Pippa's direction.

Pippa had tied bunches of sticks up and down her broom. They looked like wooden bows spaced equally apart.

"I was just . . . It was only . . ." Pippa's face flushed again. "I was just experimenting. It was only a joke." She laughed, but Trix could tell it was a fake laugh – like the way Trix's parents laughed at one of her little brother Oscar's not-funny jokes.

"I think it looks really interesting," Trix told Pippa.

"Thanks, Trix," Pippa whispered, but she ripped the bunches of twigs from her broom and tied them at the end like everyone else had done.

"Gather round, my little witches and friendly familiars," Lulu said and waved the five girls and their familiars over. Her bracelets jangled and her silvery-white hair bounced at her shoulders. "Grab your besom

and hold it out in front of
you like so." Lulu held
the broom horizontal to
the floor, which was the
wrong way for sweeping
but the right way for flying.
The girls did as Lulu instructed.

"I'm going to give you a little taste of
flying." Lulu touched each one of the girls'
broomsticks as she chanted, *"Rise up. Rise
up. One centimetre, now two. Weightless and
groundless. Let the air carry you."*

Pippa gasped as the broomsticks floated in
front of them.

"Sit on your broomstick as you would sit
on a swing," Lulu continued. "Hold on and
try to stay perfectly balanced."

Trix and the other girls climbed on their besoms. The brooms floated higher and higher. It was the strangest feeling. Trix's trainers dangled in thin air. She pointed her toes to try to touch the floor, but it was now a metre below. Pippa's broom wobbled from side to side. Trix reached out to help Pippa steady herself, but instead of steadying Pippa's broom, she unbalanced her own. Trix wobbled to one side and then leaned to the other. She knocked into Pippa's broom, Pippa floated into Stella, who grabbed Cara and Becka to keep from falling, and soon five witches and five broomsticks were piled on the floor at Lulu's feet.

"Sorry," Pippa said, tears glistening in her eyes.

"It was my fault," Trix added quickly, and maybe it was, but mostly she wanted to make Pippa feel better.

"Knowing how to fall is as important as knowing how to fly," Lulu said, smiling and reaching down to help each witch to her feet. "Everyone OK?"

"My shoes got scuffed," Stella whined, rubbing at a brown patch on her pink shoes.

"Things are not as important as people," Lulu told her. "You look practically perfect to me! Tomorrow we will have our first proper flying lesson."

Trix dusted off her school uniform. She thought of how amazing it had felt to hover even a metre in the air. Then she remembered how it had felt when she'd hit the floor with a bump. *Flying wasn't as easy as it looked!*

Chapter Two

Trix peeked under the sofa in the lounge. "Jinx, where are you?" she whispered, scanning for any trace of her sparkling black and white kitten. She tossed the lime, orange and purple throw pillows on the floor, hoping her new familiar was hiding under one of them. Jinx loved a game of hide and seek.

Trix had come right home after school. Jinx had darted into the house and now Trix couldn't find him. Trix bounced on tiptoes to see the highest shelf of the bookcase. That tiny kitten could be anywhere. Jinx magically popped here and there whenever he wanted. Maybe he was off doing witchy stuff without her.

"Have you lost your brain again, weirdo?" Oscar said as he bumped into Trix mid-jump.

Trix stumbled and knocked into the bookcase. Mum's favourite purple sculpture on the top shelf rocked back and forth. The sculpture was of an eel eating a beach ball

while twirling hula hoops. At least that's what Trix thought it looked like. Her Aunt Belle had created it in her 'artistic phase', as Dad called it. Aunt Belle had entitled it 'Purple Passion Number 46' – whatever that meant!

"Break that horrible thing and you'll be in big trouble," Oscar teased as he threw himself onto the sofa.

Trix glimpsed a flash of black and white out of the corner of her eye. She whipped around but Jinx was nowhere to be seen. Trix turned in a slow circle. That kitten must be around here somewhere.

The front door burst open. "Urgent family meeting in the lounge. Now!" Mum called.

Trix flopped down next to her brother and defended herself against his attack of elbows. "Cut it out!" Trix hissed and shoved her brother to the far end of the sofa.

"I've got some great news," Mum said, standing near the old wooden toy box that served as the Morgans' coffee table.

"Dinner's almost ready," Dad strolled into the lounge wearing his white chef's hat and an apron that had the image of a muscleman's body printed on it. "Pasta à la Rick Morgan!" Dad waved a wooden spoon, accidentally flicking bits of tomato sauce over Trix and Oscar.

Trix touched the red smudge on the collar of her school jumper and licked her finger. "You mean spag bol."

"That's like saying the Mona Lisa is just a painting," Dad protested with an exaggerated frown. "I made fresh pasta and cut it into letters. The first one to spell his or her name gets the first scoop of the Candy Bar Madness ice cream I whipped up this afternoon."

Trix licked her lips. Dad was a genius in the kitchen.

"I hope you made a few extra letters," Mum said and smiled a cheeky smile.

"How many extra letters?" Dad asked. He squinted in the way he did when he thought he wouldn't be happy with the answer.

"Just five letters," Mum replied. "An L, another L, two Es and a B."

Trix reorganised the letters in her brain.

"Belle!" she shouted. "Aunt Belle is coming for dinner!"

Next to her best friend Holly, Aunt Belle was Trix's favourite person. She travelled around the world and had had a million different jobs. She'd been a pastry chef in New York, which meant she'd only made desserts. She'd been on a dig in Egypt where they discovered some really old pots and stuff. She'd been a snowboard instructor in Switzerland, a fisherwoman in the Maldives, an artist in Paris, and a poet in Russia.

"She's not going to sleep in my room again, is she?" Oscar moaned. "I hate sleeping in the lounge."

"She can sleep with me in my room." Trix loved the idea of a sleepover with her aunt. "Why didn't you tell us sooner?"

"Well, I wanted to wait until I was sure she was coming," Mum explained. "You know your Aunt Belle can be a little . . . unpredictable."

"Fla-a-a-aaatchoo!" Dad sneezed. "Flaky," he muttered before sneezing again.

Mum's eyes narrowed at Dad like she was shooting laser beams at him, but Trix was more interested in the fact that Jinx was definitely nearby. Dad was allergic to cats. Trix tried to keep them apart but Dad would always start sneezing and sniffing when Jinx was around.

Me. Ow. Me. Me. Ow. Ow. Meow. Meow. Where was that cat? Jinx kept meowing the same rhythm over and over. It was as if he were excited too.

Trix's family didn't seem to notice the kitty cat symphony. Maybe they couldn't hear her invisible cat either! Trix looked for the source of the sound. Jinx was perched precariously on the curtain rod and eyeing Dad's chef hat, which wobbled enticingly when he sneezed. Trix could see the kitten was preparing to jump.

Atchooooo! Dad sneezed again.

Trix nudged Dad out of the way just as Jinx leaped off the curtain rod. She caught Jinx and spun around, cuddling the kitten to her chest. "Oh, please be good, Jinx,"

Trix whispered in the kitten's ear as she spun.

"What's wrong with her?" Oscar asked.
The entire Morgan family was staring at Trix.
"I told you she was crazy."

Music started to play. Trix knew that song.
It was her Aunt Belle's favourite.

"Oh, that's my mobile. It must be Belle!"
Mum's whole face seemed to glow as if she'd
swallowed the sun.

Mum answered the phone. "Hello, Belle,
is that you?" She paused, pressing the phone
to her ear. "Wait, I can't hear you. There's
what?" Mum was quiet, but she nodded and

um-ed and ah-ed. Trix could tell it wasn't good news. Mum's expression turned from sunshine to thunderstorm. "OK, no, that's fine. We'll see you in a few days."

Trix felt as if she were riding a rollercoaster. One minute she was at the tip-top of a whirly loop and the next she was plunging down, down, down.

"Sorry, Abby," Dad said to Mum when she'd hung up the phone, then he sneezed.

"It's fine. I'm fine. She's still coming. We'll have to wait a few days, that's all." Mum smiled again, but Trix could tell she was disappointed too.

Chapter Three

Jinx's spots sparkled as he followed Trix through the library the next afternoon. It was his favourite part of the day – Trix's super-secret magic lessons. Jinx marched right up to the last bookcase at the very back of the library.
He clawed at the books and wished a little bit that he could read. He knew books contained magical adventures and other things to make you smarter, but he would never understand

how those black marks on the pages made any sense at all.

"Are you ready for flying lessons?" Trix asked as the bookcase glimmered and transformed into a door.

Jinx couldn't stop nodding. He'd waited his whole kitty life to fly. He'd seen other cats sitting majestically on the back of their witches' besoms and wished for the day he'd fly like a bird through the sky.

Jinx could tell that Trix was nervous. He hadn't been her familiar very long but they already had a connection – like bumblebees and honeysuckle or yummy cream in his rumbly tummy.

The door creaked open. Jinx's whiskers twitched with the feel of fresh air and the scent of flowers. He cocked his head. It only took a second for his brain to believe what his eyes were seeing. Oh, how he loved the possibilities of magic! Impossible was nothing. But Trix's mouth gaped open. She was only a new witch. She wasn't used to the magic of magic yet.

The door in the back of the Little Witching Primary School library now led to a grassy meadow. Jinx raced from flower to flower, purple and pink and yellow and blue. Jinx inspected each colourful blossom and sniffed the sweet perfume. The sun was shining and the sky was a glorious blue. After being cramped up in school, Jinx felt as if he were flying already.

"Welcome! Welcome!" Lulu called from high above them. She was zooming through the sky on her besom with her familiar, a black cat called Sparkles, perched on the end.

Jinx marvelled at how Sparkles sat perfectly still – even when Lulu looped the loop. Jinx's paws danced with excitement.

"Magic up, my little witches," Lulu said. Trix and Jinx joined the other witches as Lulu floated down to the ground. "It's time to fly! Flying takes balance, skill, concentration and more than a little magic," Lulu said. She flicked her wrist and clicked her fingers and the besoms the girls had created yesterday appeared magically on the ground in front of them.

Trix placed Jinx on the bushy end of her broom. He wanted to look his best for his first flight, so he licked his front paw and then smoothed it over his face again and again.

Oh, Lulu is talking, Jinx realised. What have I missed? He had to learn how to pay attention because Lulu was always saying important stuff, but it wasn't easy when there were so many thoughts to think and so many things to inspect. Jinx sat up straight and pricked up his ears.

"Today I will cast a spell to help you fly," Lulu said and then quietly whispered a rhyme. The besoms rose up in the air.

Meow! Jinx exclaimed as the broom below him floated as high as Trix's waist.

"Let's start with take-offs and landings," Lulu said. "Everyone sit on your brooms. You can sit side-saddle, like sitting on a swing, or straddle the broom like riding a bike. It's up to you." Then Lulu demonstrated how to take flight – once, twice, three times. She made it look easy, gracefully slipping onto her broom side-saddle, then leaning ever so slightly forwards and pointing her toes in perfect ballerina points. Each time she smiled a wonderful glowing smile as the breeze ruffled her curls and she eased up, up and away. "My spell will allow you to fly only a few feet in the air. OK, witches, to your besoms and practise, practise, practise!"

"Here goes nothing," Trix muttered to Jinx. She climbed onto the broom like she would her bike, skipped forwards a few steps and then leaped into the air.

Jinx was sure they floated a few seconds before they tumbled to the ground. Jinx shook the dirt off his fur.

"I'll get better," Trix promised him.

Jinx brushed up against Trix's leg before hopping onto the back of the broom again. He wanted to show that he believed in her.

Trix tried hopping and skipping and jumping, but each take-off ended in a bumpy and almost immediate landing. Luckily, the meadow was a forgiving place for flying lessons. The soft grasses cushioned each mishap.

Jinx watched the other witches. Everyone was having the same problem. Witches and familiars were spending more time on the ground than in the air. But everyone was levitating a little bit – except Pippa and Twitch. It was as if Pippa's feet were glued to the ground. Jinx felt sorry for her.

"Come on, Jinx!" Trix called. Jinx scampered over and hopped onto the broom. Trix's eyebrows scrunched together and her forehead wrinkled. She was really concentrating. "OK, we are going to do it this time. Think of flying!"

Jinx thought of bluebottles, bumblebees, butterflies and birds. He thought of flapping wings and floating clouds and he even thought of himself when he jumped into Trix's arms. She was going to do it this time. He wiggled his whiskers to give her a Jinx Jingle Jangle magical boost.

"Ready! Steady! GO!" Trix shouted. She leaned forwards and lifted one foot off the ground and then the other. "We're doing it, Jinx!" Trix exclaimed.

The broom lurched. Both Trix and Jinx clung on. And then they were flying. They weren't far off the ground but, still, they were flying. "Hang on!" Trix shouted as the broom jerked forwards.

"Well done, my little witches!" Lulu called and clapped her hands. Stella, Cara and Becka were airborne too.

"Me . . . me . . . me . . . wowowowow!" screeched Jinx. His stomach seemed to somersault in his body as Trix's broom zigzagged through the air.

"Creeping cats!" Trix exclaimed. "How do I turn this thing, Jinx? We are heading straight for that . . . that . . . that . . ."

Trix didn't need to finish her sentence. Jinx could see the big pine tree dead ahead. It seemed to him that the tree was heading straight for THEM.

"Hold on tight!" Trix screamed and pulled back as hard as she could on the broom. Now they were heading straight up. Jinx pressed himself flat, wrapping all four legs around the broom handle. He closed his eyes. In his experience, sometimes it was better not to look.

The broom levelled and their pace slowed. When he felt brave enough, Jinx opened one eye and then the other. He looked down and saw clouds and blue sky. What? Jinx blinked and looked again. This time he saw Stella and Rascal floating upside down. Something is higgledy-piggledy, Jinx thought. He glanced at Trix. Her hair was standing on end and brushing the tall grasses as they skimmed across the meadow. That's when he realised ... Stella and Rascal were right-side up. He and Trix were flying upside down!

"Try a spell!" Lulu called to Trix.

Trix chanted the same spell over and over, "Flying's not going as I planned. I need magic to help me land!"

"That was amazing," Pippa said as Trix and Jinx turned right side up and glided in to land. "I never left the ground. You are definitely the best at flying."

"It was . . ." Trix started. She took a deep breath. She was as white as a bowl of milk. "It was super and duper." Trix said at last. "And a little bit scary."

Stella landed her besom right in between Trix and Pippa. "How was flying for you, Pippa?" Stella said with a mocking edge to her voice.

Oh, that Stella is so mean! Jinx thought of her as a pink lizard. She was always saying unkind things. Maybe she was cold-blooded like a real lizard.

Stella opened her mouth. Jinx could see by the look in her beady eyes that she was going to say something mean again. But before she could utter one nasty syllable, Lulu's voice rang out.

"Wonderful first flights, my little witches. Pippa,

I got the SENSE of flight,
just not the height. You'll
get there, my darling.
It's not about being
first or best but
being yourself! Your
homework . . ." The
witches groaned and
Lulu laughed. "Magic
homework is never
dull," she told them. "I
want you to create
an incantation for
flying."

"In-can-what?" Pippa
asked, reaching down to
let Twitch scamper up her arm and perch
on her shoulder. The rat sniffled the air as if
wondering what Lulu's big word meant too.

"An incantation is a special spell you will use
every time you fly," Lulu replied. "You will say
it before you take flight. It's unique to each witch,
so you will need to experiment – in secret, of
course." Lulu flicked her wrist and clicked her

fingers and they were back in the magic classroom. "Have a magical weekend and I'll see you on Monday!"

Chapter Four

"When is Aunt Belle coming?" Trix asked the moment Mum walked into the kitchen the next morning. Waiting was worse than taking tests or eating Brussels sprouts or even taking tests while being force-fed Brussels sprouts.

Trix had woken up early, even though it was Saturday, and had made herself a bowl of her favourite chocolatey cereal. Her brain was filled with thoughts of seeing Aunt Belle. Aunt Belle was as wonderful as Mum with the fun parts of Holly wrapped in a crazy, unpredictable bow.

Thump! Thump! Thump! It was the distinct sound of Oscar as he bounded down the stairs. He had a way of making everything as noisy as possible.

Mum rubbed her eyes and took a seat next to Trix at the kitchen table. "Your Aunt Belle said she would arrive tomorrow, but you know Aunt Belle . . ." Mum's voice trailed off.

"Aunt Belle is great, but she's weird just like Trix," Oscar said as he shuffled into the room. "It must be in the name."

Trix glared at Oscar. She and her aunt shared the same magical name – Trixibelle – but Aunt Belle used the last part as her nickname and Trix used the first.

Knock! Knock!

Mum looked at Oscar.

Knock! Knock! The sound came again.

Oscar raised his hands. "It's not me!"

"Special delivery for Trixibelle and Oscar Morgan," a voice called through the letterbox.

Trix and Oscar raced to the front door, bouncing into each other like pinballs as they sped down the hall. When they opened the door, a delivery man was standing there, holding two boxes wrapped in brown paper. He handed one to Trix and one to Oscar. Trix loved getting packages in the post, but she had never, ever received anything by special delivery before. Mum had to sign for each package, which made them super-duper special.

Trix turned her box over and over. "Look!" she said and pointed at the postmark. "It says it's come all the way from Australia. These must be from Aunt Belle!"

"She really shouldn't spoil you kids," Mum murmured, but the smile on her face said that maybe Aunt Belle wasn't so bad after all.

Oscar ripped open his package right there in the hall, but Trix took hers into the lounge. Her fingers itched to rip open the package, but she liked to take her time and enjoy the anticipation. She took a deep breath and slowly peeled back the tape that secured the wrapping.

"Look what I got!" Oscar shouted and burst into the lounge.

"Keep your voice down! Your father is still sleeping," Mum said.

"Not any more!" Dad shouted from upstairs.

"It's a thingy whatsit!" Oscar waved a V-shaped piece of wood like a sword over his head.

"That's a boomerang," Trix told him. "You throw it and it comes right back to you."

Oscar looked at Mum to

make sure Trix wasn't telling a fib, which she wasn't. She didn't know how it worked, but she knew that's what boomerangs were supposed to do.

Trix carefully opened her box. Inside there was a bright orange envelope on top of another package wrapped in paper covered with kittens and cats. Aunt Belle knew her so well. Trix read the card: *Good luck with flying! Remember to enjoy it!*

Flying? After her performance yesterday, she needed all the luck she could get, but Aunt Belle couldn't know that Trix had started flying lessons. No one outside the Sisterhood of Magic knew Trix was a witch. What a funny coincidence!

Trix couldn't stand the suspense any longer. She ripped open the package and shreds of paper flew in every direction.

"A kite!" Trix exclaimed, lifting it out of the box. It was all the colours of the rainbow. There wasn't a picture on it exactly, but Trix could see a million different things mixed up in the crazy image. If she turned her head this

way there was a pink
bird with purple
spots, but if she
tilted her head and
squinted just so, then
she saw a school of
tropical fish swimming
in a sea of orange squash.

"Can Holly and I go to the
park, Mum?" Trix begged. She and Holly
spent every Saturday together and flying her
brand new kite would be the perfect way
to pass the day. "Pretty please with sugar,
sprinkles and chocolate ripple fudge on the
top!"

"Only if you take Oscar with you," Mum
replied.

Oscar was swinging the boomerang like
a cricket bat, only just missing the family
picture hanging on the wall.

"Oscar!" Mum yelled. "Put that away until
you are outside."

"Aw, Mum!" Oscar whined.

"Do I have to take him?" Trix asked, but

she already knew the answer. That was the curse of the big sister. Wherever she went, her little brother came too.

Trix held tight to the string while Holly raised the kite over her head. The park was right next to Little Witching Primary School and it was jam-packed with families and pets, enjoying the Saturday sunshine.

"Ready! Steady! Go!" Holly called.

Trix took off running. The kite soared up, up, up. Trix released more string little by little and let the kite fly higher and higher. Holly came racing over and they watched as the rainbow-coloured kite painted pictures among the clouds.

"Your aunt gives the best gifts!" Holly said without taking her eyes off the kite. "I wish I had an Aunt Belle."

Trix thought Holly was lucky in some ways – she didn't have any pesky brothers and sisters. But she didn't have any aunts or uncles either – which Trix thought was a bit unlucky.

As Trix watched her kite, she thought about flying on her besom. Trix let the wind take the kite where it wanted. She only

needed to tug the string lightly this way to make the kite zoom to the left, and a little tug that way made it swoop right. Trix felt as if she and the kite were dancing, swaying together and responding to each other. Maybe that was the trick to flying. Maybe she needed to stop thinking so hard about it and just enjoy the feeling.

"The colours on the kite seem to be swirling," Holly said. Trix squinted up. Holly was right. The colours seemed to change and shift as the kite flew higher and higher. But that was impossible.

Suddenly the kite seemed to stop in mid-air. "Oscar!" Trix shouted as her beautiful kite was struck by a boomerang and crashed to the ground.

Chapter Five

"Flight. Bright. Kite. Height," Trix sang as she lined up Jinx and her twenty-three toy cats on her bed on Sunday morning. The sun was up but no one else in the Morgan house was awake yet. It was the perfect time for a little flying practice.

"Knight. Light. Quite. Right." The words trickled off her tongue.

She had to come up with her flying

incantation. Rhyming wasn't hard. She'd thought of loads of rhyming words, but she couldn't come up with a spell. She couldn't very well go zipping around her room on a broom, so she'd had the brilliant idea of flying cats!

She set her favourite cuddly black cat on her pillow. Holly had given her this toy last year on their BFF-versary. Trix and Holly had been best friends for ever, but they declared the day that was halfway between their birthdays as their official BFF-versary. It was another excuse to give each other gifts. Trix glared at the stuffed cat.

"Flying high, in the sky," Trix whispered. That was a good start for her spell, but now her mind went blank. What rhymed with fly,

high and *sky*? "*Why-o-why-o-why-o-why!*"
It rhymed, but the cat didn't move.

Maybe that was too many rhymes. She
cleared her throat and tried again. "*Think of
floating and being light,*" she began, pointing
at the little purple and green plastic cat that
Oscar had found in the park. It hadn't been a
gift exactly. It had been covered in mud and
he'd dropped it into her lemonade. "*But this
spell isn't right,*" Trix finished.

She groaned and threw herself on the bed
next to Jinx. He blended in with the other
cats on her duvet until he curved his paw over
his eyes.

"Are you trying to make me disappear?"
Trix asked. Jinx opened one eye and cocked
his head as if to say, *Don't be silly.*

"OK. OK. Think! Think! Think!" she told herself.

She remembered flying her beautiful kite with Holly yesterday – before Oscar's stupid boomerang had destroyed it. Dad had tried to patch it up, but it didn't look the same covered in shiny tape. Trix flipped onto her back and stared up at the ceiling. She imagined herself zooming among the clouds like her kite.

"Floating. Flitting. Lighter than air," Trix said. *"Flying is easy when you haven't a care."*

Trix pointed to each of her cats. And one by one they slowly rose from the bed and drifted gently, higher and higher. Trix stifled a squeal of excitement. She didn't want to wake her family, but her incantation had worked!

Trix scooped up Jinx and stood on her bed. She twirled Jinx around among the floating cats. She kissed

him on the head and repeated
the incantation. When she
opened her arms, he floated
away! His wide yellow eyes
stared at her in disbelief and
then with a happy *meow* he
started to control his flight. He was an
expert pilot. He waved his paws
and whipped his tail from
side to side.

"Jinx, the super cat!"
Trix said as she watched
her now sparkling, purring
cat zigzagging around her
room. Then she pointed at her toy cats
and, with a flick of her finger, she sent each
one floating in a different direction.

Oh, this is so much fun! It was
like a ballet of flying cats. She
bounced on the bed. Jinx
zoomed by one cat and then
another.

"Trix! Oscar!" Mum called.
"Time to get up!"

Trix's flying fun was over. Trix grabbed for one cat and then another, but they slipped out of her grasp. It was as if some strange gravity were pulling them up instead of down.

"But, Mum," Trix heard Oscar whine from his room. "It's Sunday!"

"I know," Mum called, "but Aunt Belle emailed and she's flying in this afternoon. We need to get ready so we can pick her up from the airport."

Aunt Belle was finally coming!

"Trix, you need to tidy up," Mum went on, her voice getting louder, "if you want Aunt Belle to stay in your room with you." Trix heard the distinct sound of Mum's steps on the landing and realised she had to do something fast! Mum was coming to her room. How would she ever explain twenty-four flying cats?

Chapter Six

"Creeping cats!" Trix whispered. She told her brain to think of a spell that would ground her flying cats. What was the opposite of flying?

Trix uttered the first rhyme that came into her mind. "*Flying's fun. What a great time I've had. But it's time to land so Mum won't get mad.*"

"Trix?" Mum said and knocked on the door.

As the door slowly opened, all twenty-three of Trix's cats came crashing down. She covered her head to keep from being battered. Jinx dived straight for Trix's pillow and landed with a soft *kerplop!*

"Oh, Trix!" Mum exclaimed.

"What?" Trix asked, scanning the ceiling for flying cats.

"Your room is such a mess!" Mum said, picking up a few of the toy cats that were now scattered on the floor. Mum was right. Her room looked like a battleground after a war of cats.

Trix gave a sheepish smile and shrugged. She couldn't explain about her flying incantation because Mum didn't know her daughter was a witch. "I'll clean it all up, Mum," Trix said, scooping up an armful of toys. "And I'll be ready before you can say 'abracadabra'." Trix grinned and wished Lulu had taught them a clean-up spell!

All it took was an emergency call to Holly, and both Trix and her room were ready in no time. During the long and very non-magical car ride to the airport, Trix wished she could cast a flying spell on her family's tired old car. It didn't help that Oscar thought pinching and poking Trix and Holly was the best way to pass the time, but finally they arrived thirty-two minutes before Aunt Belle's plane was scheduled to land.

Mum checked her watch and then the huge TV screens giving flight details. Trix studied the lists of places she'd never been and hoped some day she and Holly would be at the airport for *Departures* instead of *Arrivals*.

"Tell me another Aunt Belle story," Holly begged.

Trix thought for a second. She'd already told Holly about Aunt Belle meeting the Queen and Aunt Belle's ability to say the alphabet as quickly backwards as forwards. "Aunt Belle was once a singing rodeo clown named Cow Belle. She's also been a personal shopper in Milan, a truck driver in Alaska and a trapeze artist in Berlin."

"You've got to be joking!" Holly said. Her red curls bounced as she giggle-snorted.

"You can ask Mum," Trix said and pulled Holly out of the way of a family pushing a trolley overflowing with suitcases. When Trix grew up she wanted to be just like her Aunt Belle and travel the world having amazing adventures.

"Her flight has landed," Mum said. There was always a lightness about Mum when her little sister came to visit. While Aunt Belle was here, Mum would seem more like a sister than a mum.

Mum led Trix and Holly to the *Arrivals* hall. Shiny silver barriers kept families and friends away from the arriving passengers. Trix thought it looked like a corral for horses. She grabbed Holly's hand and ducked under waving arms until they were at the very front.

"Look!" Holly pointed.

Trix's stomach hiccupped with excitement. Had Holly spotted Aunt Belle?

"Look at those two blokes wearing cowboy hats," Holly said. "Do you think they've been to the Wild West?"

Trix imagined herself and Holly riding horses across a rocky plain. Maybe they would capture masked bandits. Were there still masked bandits in the Wild West?

"I wonder where *these* guys have been," Trix whispered to Holly as a group of seven men passed, carrying heavy bags and puffy coats.

"I think they've hiked up . . ." Holly squinted as if she were thinking really, really hard. "What's that huge mountain people climb?"

"Mount Everest," Trix said. "Let's climb that together some day!"

"No way!" Holly said. Her *thinking* face

changed to her *you're crazy* face. Trix had seen that face many times before. "It's freezing up there. Let's go to the beach."

"And swim with sharks or scuba dive for treasure ships?" Trix asked. She bounced on her toes as a million ideas popped into her head of all the places she and Holly could go.

"No," Holly quickly corrected. "We could lie on the beach in really cute bikinis!"

Trix shook her head and laughed. She and her friend had very different ideas about adventure.

While they waited for Aunt Belle, Trix and Holly continued to play their guessing game, Trix imagining action and adventure and Holly dreaming of glamorous getaways. Behind them, Mum kept rising up on tiptoe to study each new batch of passengers as they streamed through the electronic doors.

Trix's legs were getting tired and her excitement faded with each passing minute. *Will Aunt Belle ever get here?* Then she had a terrible thought. She glanced up at Mum and she knew she was having the same thought too. *What if Aunt Belle missed her plane? What if she isn't coming?* It had happened once before.

"Trix! Trix!" Holly was tugging on Trix's shirt. Trix didn't feel like playing any more. "Trix!" Holly's voice was louder. "That's her, isn't it?"

Trix followed Holly's gaze and immediately spotted her favourite aunt. "Aunt Belle! Over here!" Trix shouted and waved wildly.

And it was as if the brightest spotlight had been turned onto Aunt Belle as she waved back. She was like a rock star, fashion model and chat show hostess rolled into one. She had short, spiky blonde hair with streaks of hot pink that were new since last time Trix had seen her. Her ears twinkled with several earrings. She wore a short, twirly skirt, fancy, high-heeled boots and a blouse that had multi-coloured sequins all over it so that she glittered in the airport lights.

Another flash of sparkles caught Trix's eye. It was Jinx! When had he shown up? Her delightfully crazy familiar always knew exactly where she was. It was part of the magical connection between witch and familiar. Jinx raced from behind the barrier. Trix reached for him, but it was too late. He dashed out of her grasp and ran straight for Aunt Belle. He was dodging trainers and high heels and skidding and sliding on the tile floor.

"Trixibelle!" Aunt Belle shouted and raced towards Trix, struggling under the weight of many mismatched bags. Trix cringed as her favourite aunt and invisible familiar headed straight for each other. She imagined the horrible collision that was bound to come next – arms and legs windmilling in the air, followed by a shower of bags and fur!

Trix raised her hand and opened her mouth to yell but, just in the nick of time, Aunt Belle side-stepped out of Jinx's path. Trix

ARRIVALS

	10.00
	10.10
	10.15
	10.30
	11.15
	11.40
	12.00

laughed with relief as the kitten tumbled out of the way.

Aunt Belle wrapped her arms around Trix and gave her the biggest hug. Trix hugged her right back. Aunt Belle had arrived at last!

Chapter Seven

Jinx thought Monday was always the longest day of the school week, and he was relieved when it was time for another magical lesson from Lulu. Lulu had taken her witches-in-training to the enchanted meadow for their first proper flights. There would be no magical assistance from Lulu this time. She'd instructed the familiars to watch from the big oak tree on the edge of the meadow.

Because the girls would be trying out their flying

incantations for the first
time, Lulu had decided it
was best for the
familiars to watch
their witches
until she was
sure their flying
spells worked,
and had declared
them safe for
flight. Sherlock the owl
flapped over to join Jinx
and Tabby the cat, who were
perched on a branch near
the top.

Sherlock hooted and
swivelled his head to follow
his witch Becka, who was
already flying but
only seemed to
be able to go
round and
round
the tree.

Jinx was beginning to think maybe she was stuck in a permanent left turn. Stella's pug, Rascal, and Twitch the rat were resting at the base of the trunk.

Jinx wiggled his whiskers and sent all his magical thoughts Trix's way. He heard her recite her flying incantation and saw her lean forwards. And then Trix's besom lifted off the ground almost as neatly and smoothly as Lulu's had done in her demonstration. Trix was flying under the power of her own magic! Trix and broom glided forwards. She was staying low and floating more than flying. The ribbons on her tiny witch's hat flapped behind her like streamers. Trix waved as she passed the oak tree and Jinx felt very proud.

"A little too high!" Lulu called to Stella who was already whizzing over the treetops. "And nothing fancy."

"I'm fine, miss!" Stella tipped her witch's hat in what might have been a gesture of respect but Jinx thought Stella was being rude. "My mum and grandmama are great at flying. They gave me a few tips – and, obviously, I've got natural talent."

Cara zoomed up beside Stella. She pointed down to the ground and then the girls started to giggle. Jinx hated that noise. It sounded the way wet fur felt. Jinx looked to where Cara had pointed. Poor Pippa was bouncing up and down on her broom. Lulu had zapped a training bubble around Pippa to protect her, but she'd still managed to skin both her knees when she'd tried to land.

"Keep trying, Pippa!" Lulu shouted. "You're improving!"

Jinx couldn't wait any longer. He was desperate to fly with Trix. He raised a paw towards Lulu, lifted his chin and meowed with all his might.

"You are right, Jinx Jingle Jangle," Lulu called to him. "Trix is ready for a passenger. Her magic is working, well, magically!" Lulu waved Trix over. "Why don't you take Jinx on a quick flight around the meadow? Don't be afraid to fly a bit higher this time, but not too fast," she told Trix.

Trix beamed. She flew over and hovered next to Jinx's tree branch. Jinx stretched his paw onto the bushy end of the broom to test it. Trix held the broom perfectly still and Jinx climbed aboard. Trix angled the broom higher and off they went. "Isn't this fun?" Trix asked Jinx. His tummy had gone all wiggle-worms and buzzing bees. He had never flown this high before. He wondered if this was what birds felt like.

"Creeping cats!" Trix said and pointed her broom back down to the meadow. Jinx spotted it too. Stella and Cara had landed on either side of Pippa's training bubble. He couldn't hear what they were saying but he could tell by Pippa's frown that it wasn't very nice. Lulu was too busy chasing Sherlock, who was himself chasing a runaway Becka, to notice Stella's mean behaviour.

Trix flew a tight circle around Pippa's bubble, which forced Stella and Cara to stumble backwards to keep from being knocked over by Trix's broom.

"Oh, sorry!" Trix called as she landed next to Pippa, but Jinx could tell Trix wasn't sorry and it wasn't an accident. Trix was flying to Pippa's rescue and Jinx loved her just a little bit more for it.

"Watch what you're doing!" Stella shrieked.

"Yeah, watch it!" Cara echoed. She always seemed to mimic Stella. Jinx felt sorry for anyone who didn't know how to think for themselves.

Stella pointed the sharp end of her broom at Pippa's training bubble and it burst with an almighty pop! "Bye, bye, bubble girl!" Stella said and then with a hop, skip and a jump, Stella and Cara jetted back into the air.

"Don't worry about them," Trix said and helped Pippa wipe the slimy bubble goo from her hair. "You'll get the hang of flying soon."

"I think it might be my incantation," Pippa said. "Maybe I could use yours. Mine's rubbish."

"I don't think that's how it works," Trix said. "Lulu said we should each have our own incantation. But maybe I could help you with the rhyming bit. I'm pretty good at it. Try me. Say any word and I'll come up with a word that rhymes!"

"Lavender," Pippa said, giving Twitch a little wave.

Trix puckered her lips and squinted her eyes, trying to think of any words that rhymed with lavender. "Oh, that's too difficult," she decided in the end. "How about rat?" she suggested, then blurted, "Rat. Hat. Sat. Bat. Cat. Lat. Mat. Zat . . ." On and on Trix went, and the crazier the words, the bigger Pippa's smile became.

"Magic up, my little witches!" Lulu clapped her hands. "I have a lovely surprise for my newly airborne pupils."

"Not all of us were airborne," Jinx heard Stella whisper to Cara. "Some of us fly like stones."

Jinx sprang from Trix's broom and hissed at Stella in disgust.

Stella flinched. "Can't you control your cat?" she asked Trix.

"Can't you control your tongue?" was Trix's reply. She winked at Jinx and he winked back.

When witches and familiars had gathered round, Lulu shared her surprise. "On Friday I will take you on a special midnight flight." Jinx's tail twitched with excitement at the thought. "And I will introduce each of you to your very own magical mentor."

"What's a mentor?" Pippa asked. Jinx loved that Pippa wasn't scared to ask questions. He thought that was very brave.

"A mentor is a cross between a friend and a teacher," Lulu explained. "All the mentors are first-class fairy godmothers. They will answer your questions and help guide you as you learn to control your magic, and, I hope, become fairy godmothers one day."

"Mine will probably be a princess or maybe a fashion designer," Stella proclaimed. She cupped her hand and whispered in Pippa's ear. "Yours is probably a dustbin woman!"

Lulu stepped in front of Stella. "What is wrong with a dustbin woman?" she asked, looking down her nose and right into Stella's eyes.

"Um, n-nothing, m-miss," Stella stammered. "I was just—"

"Well, don't!" Lulu interrupted. "If you want to be a fairy godmother some day, you will remember that every person is special."

"Yes, miss." Stella's shoulders sagged and she looked at the ground.

"Now where was I?" Lulu moved into the centre of the circle again. "Oh, yes! Magical mentors. Practise your flying so you will be ready for our marvellous mystery flight on Friday."

Jinx leaped into Trix's arms, spots sparkling. What could be more magical than a midnight flight?

Chapter Eight

A s soon as Lulu transported them back
to the magic classroom, Stella, Cara and
Becka dashed away, whispering and giggling.
Trix had loved flying, but she was anxious to
get home. Having Aunt Belle at home while
she was at school was like having an Easter
basket full of sweets and a tummy ache. Aunt
Belle had promised to make fairy cakes with
Trix and Holly after school.

Trix scooped up Jinx and started to leave when she noticed Pippa lingering near Lulu's bookcase full of magical ingredients. Her shoulders were shaking. Trix knew she was crying.

"What's the matter?" Trix asked, but she already knew. Stella had focused all her nasty attention on Pippa today. Trix knew how that felt. Usually Trix was the punchline to Stella's mean jokes.

"Stella is right. I'm rubbish at flying." Pippa sniffed and wiped her eyes. "I'll never become a fairy godmother."

"Yes, you will!" Trix said. "We're still learning and everyone has different talents. You were really good at making things disappear, remember? You'll learn to fly. It just takes practice." She hated to see Pippa so sad. Suddenly the most brilliant idea popped into Trix's brain. "I know one fairy thing you'd be great at!"

"What's that?" Pippa asked as Trix guided her out of the library.

"Decorating fairy cakes!" Trix replied. "My

aunt, my friend, Holly, and I are going to make..." Trix grinned, "... and *eat* loads of fairy cakes. Why don't you join us?"

"I *do* like fairy cakes," Pippa said with the hint of a smile.

Trix could smell smoke as soon as she opened the front door. She rushed to the kitchen followed by Holly and Pippa. Pippa's mum had been happy to let Pippa come over. She'd even dropped them off in front of Trix's house after school. Jinx and Twitch had stayed behind to help with what Lulu called 'magical search and discover', but Trix suspected she meant a game of hide and seek.

"Nothing to worry about," Aunt Belle sing-songed as she flapped a kitchen towel at the smoke billowing from the oven. "Just a minor baking mishap. Burning one batch is a sign of good luck!" Even smudged with flour, her aunt looked glamorous with her blonde spiky hairstyle and a bright, glittery pink T-shirt that matched the stripes in her hair.

"I didn't know that!" Pippa exclaimed. "My mum says burning stuff is a sign that I'm not paying attention. She says I'm always daydreaming, but that's not true, I'm usually—"

"What stinks?" Oscar burst through the back door with a jar full of bugs. "Trix must be cooking!" He skidded to a muddy stop when he spotted Pippa. "Oh, hi," Oscar

mumbled and Trix thought he was blushing under the layer of dirt on his cheeks.

"Pippa," Trix said and touched the sleeve of Pippa's purple and pink school uniform, "this is my Aunt Belle and my brother Oscar."

"Pleased to meet you," Pippa said and air-kissed Aunt Belle's cheek. She waved to Oscar who was studying the creepy-crawlies he'd captured in his jar. Trix couldn't believe it, but Oscar was actually speechless.

Aunt Belle placed the fairy-cake pan from the smoking oven on top of the hob. Trix wrinkled her nose at the burnt smell wafting from what looked like six lumps of coal in silver foil wrappers. "Never mind," Aunt Belle said, ushering the group to the kitchen table. "My baking hasn't been a complete failure." Rows and rows of vanilla and chocolate fairy cakes dotted the table.

Oscar reached for a chocolate one. "We have to decorate them first," Aunt Belle said and rapped Oscar's hand lightly.

"Can I help?" he asked, looking from the fairy cakes to Pippa.

"No!" Trix blurted. This was her special time with her friends and Aunt Belle. Oscar would find a way to ruin everything and embarrass her at the same time. He always did.

Aunt Belle draped her arm around Trix's shoulders. "Maybe we could let him help for a little while."

Trix shrugged but glared at Oscar. He placed his bug jar on the kitchen counter and wiped his muddy hands on his already mucky school uniform. He gave Trix a cheeky look that she knew meant she'd need to watch him like a hawk, two hawks – a whole flock of hawks, really.

"Oscar, if you want to help you need to wash your hands. And please release those poor bugs outside where you found them!" Aunt Belle said. "How would you like it if I trapped you in a jar?"

Trix smirked. She quite liked the thought of capturing Oscar in a humungous jar. It was the only way he would ever stay out of trouble.

"Now, unleash your imaginations," Aunt Belle said when Oscar had freed the bugs in the garden and washed his hands. "It's time to decorate!" She opened a bright yellow bag. "Here are a few things I collected on my travels." She handed Holly some tubs of icing and Pippa three tiny pots of multi-coloured sprinkles. "Let the magic begin!"

Trix and Pippa shared a sneaky secret smile. They knew a little something about magic.

Trix was experimenting with mixing sprinkles and pastel-coloured sugar flakes into creamy vanilla icing. It looked pretty and tasted great on her fingers. Pippa did the same. Then Aunt Belle created a red rose out of icing. So did Pippa. Holly made sugary pink and green polka-dots on the top of another fairy cake. Pippa did too.

Aunt Belle's mobile phone rang with what sounded like the bongs of Big Ben. "Oh, sorry," she said, checking the screen. "Duty calls. I need to take this." She stepped into the lounge to answer it.

When Oscar thought no one was looking, he pulled a bug from his pocket, covered it in green icing, and plopped it onto Holly's polka-dot fairy cake. But Trix had spotted his mischief and snatched the bug-topped cake away. Oscar was not going to embarrass her in front of Pippa. Oscar grabbed for the bug-topped cake, knocking it out of Trix's hand.

"Drat and double drat!" Holly exclaimed when she saw her fairy cake splatter on the floor.

"Sorry, Holly!" Trix said, wiping up the crumbly, sticky, buggy mess. "You'll just have to make another one."

Oscar slipped a pot of glittery sugar off the table and started rummaging around in one of the kitchen cabinets. *Ignore him*, Trix told herself, determined not to let Oscar ruin all the fun. But the more he messed about, the more nervous Trix got. *What is he doing?* she wondered.

"What should I use on this one?" Holly

asked and held up a fairy cake with swirly yellow icing on top.

"Sprinkle it with this!" Oscar said and handed Holly the glittery sugar pot he'd taken earlier.

"Let's sprinkle it on all the cakes," Pippa said, shaking the glittery sugar on top of all the fairy cakes they'd just finished decorating.

Trix picked up the sugar pot as soon as Pippa set it down on the table. She sprinkled some in her palm and licked it off. *Creeping cats!* her taste buds squealed. Oscar had put salt in the sugar container. Before she could say anything, she noticed her aunt watching from the doorway. Had she seen Oscar's trick?

"Wow! You've done a marvellous job," Aunt Belle piped up, strolling over to the fairy-cake-topped kitchen table. "Our work is done. What a tasty treat! No mistakes here. Now we eat!" She picked up a fairy cake and took a huge bite. Before Trix could stop them, Holly and Pippa did the same. Oscar started to giggle.

"These taste amazing!" Pippa said, her mouth smeared with glittery icing.

"You make the best fairy cakes on the planet!" Holly agreed, licking her lips. "Maybe the whole galaxy!"

How can they taste good when they are covered in salt? Trix wondered. She tasted a fingerful of the salt-topped icing. "This does taste great!" she exclaimed in surprise and finished the icing *and* another fairy cake.

"What?" Oscar looked disappointed.

"These are magical," Pippa said, winking at Trix and making her wonder if perhaps Pippa had seen Oscar switch the pots and then used her magic to save the cakes. Now Pippa was all icing sugar and smiles. Any hint of her earlier sadness had vanished – like the salt on the top of the fairy cakes.

Chapter Nine

Trix's stomach felt as if she'd swallowed one of those topsy-turvy rides at a village fête. After Pippa had gone home, Aunt Belle had cooked dinner for the Morgan family and Holly too. She'd called it a *vegetarian taste-bud explosion*. Trix had never had macaroni and cheese with jalapeno peppers, nor had she tasted anything like spinach soup or cheddar-and-garlic bread

rolls. Aunt Belle had brought olives from
Spain and cheeses from France. Trix loved to
try new things, but maybe trying them all at
once hadn't been a great idea.

"Why don't we clear away the dishes?"
Dad said to Trix and Holly. "Oscar, you get
ready for bed. It's almost your bedtime.
Let's let your mum and Aunt Belle catch
up." Dad stacked the plates into one tall
tower.

"But, Dad . . ." Trix started, but she didn't
have a good reason for not helping. "Come
on, Holly."

Oscar moaned and groaned and stamped all
the way up the stairs.

When the table was cleared, Dad made
himself a sandwich of ham and left-over
chicken. "Let's keep this our secret," he told
Trix and Holly, "but I don't call it dinner
without meat." He sneaked out to the back
garden to eat.

Trix and Holly made a game of washing up
which ended in a soap suds fight. Soon they
were covered in blobs of froth. "We look like

a couple of fairy cakes now!" Trix laughed
and Holly giggle-snorted.

They heard Mum and Aunt Belle's laughter
echoing from the lounge. "Don't you wish
we had sisters?" Holly asked.

"We've got each other," Trix said, giving
Holly a hug. "Let's swear to be as close as
sisters always."

"I swear!" Holly said and crossed her heart
and hooked little fingers with Trix. That was
how they always sealed their promises to
each other.

"Let's go up to my room and you can
show me another of your magic tricks," Trix
said when they'd finished clearing up. Holly

wanted to be a world-famous magician. She practised all the time and was getting better and better.

As they reached the top of the stairs, the girls heard Aunt Belle exclaim, "Abby, really! You don't understand." She didn't sound happy.

Trix pressed a finger to her lips to beg Holly to keep quiet and crept back down the stairs. Mum and Aunt Belle never fought. Something must be wrong.

"You are going to have to settle down some time." Mum's voice sounded cross, as if she were correcting Oscar. "You can't keep flitting about from job to job. I worry about you."

"But, Abby, I'm happy," Aunt Belle protested.

"Why are you going to London?" Mum asked, and it suddenly sounded to Trix like one of those TV shows where a police officer tries to get a criminal to confess.

"Oh, for this and that," Aunt Belle said, her voice higher than normal. "You know me!"

Trix didn't like that her mum and aunt were arguing. It made her feel a little sad inside.

"No, Trixibelle, that's just it. I don't think I *do* know you any more." Mum's voice sounded more sad than angry now. "I miss you."

"You don't have to worry about me, sis," Aunt Belle said.

Trix peeked around the corner. They were hugging. Perhaps everything was going to be OK. But something still wasn't right. Trix could feel it. Maybe it was part of her new magicalness, but she felt as if Aunt Belle were hiding something. She hoped her aunt wasn't in any trouble.

"Mum! Mum!" Oscar shouted and squashed Trix against the wall on his way down the stairs. "Trix and Holly were eavesdropping! They're right here hiding!"

"Trix? Holly?" Mum's voice sounded annoyed again.

Trix and Holly walked the rest of the way down the stairs and into the lounge. Trix couldn't look at Mum or Aunt Belle.

"What were you doing on the stairs?"
Mum asked.

"Well, I heard . . ." Trix didn't really want
to say. She knew she shouldn't have been
listening. "I heard you arguing."

Now Mum looked as if she were the one
who'd got caught doing something she
shouldn't. "Everything is fine. Your aunt and
I were just having a disagreement," Mum said
and then regained her mum-ishness. "But you
know it's not nice to listen to other people's
conversations."

"I know," Trix said. "I'm sorry."

"All's forgiven," Aunt Belle replied. Trix
thought maybe Aunt Belle was talking to her
and Mum. "How about another fairy cake?"

Trix, Holly and Oscar dashed into the kitchen before Mum overruled Aunt Belle's suggestion. Trix wasn't sure a fairy cake could make her feel better, though. She didn't like the feeling of being in trouble or of knowing something she shouldn't. Also, she didn't know why exactly, but something was still worrying her about her favourite aunt.

Chapter Ten

Today Lulu had transported her witches to an abandoned airfield. Old planes were scattered along the cracked runway. There were small one-person planes and bigger passenger planes with propellers. All of them were rusty and banged-up and looked as if they'd been planted in a weed-filled garden. Trix imagined the places those planes had been.

"We're going to try a test flight together," Lulu said, landing gracefully just like Trix had seen planes do when they'd picked up Aunt Belle from the airport. "This new location is for our more serious flights!" Trix glanced over at Pippa. Her purple and pink Enchanted Grove school uniform was smudged with dirt and twigs were stuck in her droopy blonde ponytail. Lulu had given Pippa an extra lesson before the other girls arrived, but it looked as if Pippa had spent more time on the ground than she had in the air.

"Psst!" Stella beckoned Pippa over. "Here!" She shoved a piece of paper into Pippa's hand. "It's obvious you're having problems flying. Why don't you use my flying incantation? As you know," Stella said, climbing onto her broom and flicking her perfectly straightened hair over her shoulder, "I'm the best flyer here."

"Oh, thanks, Stella!" Pippa smiled. She unfolded the paper and whispered the rhyme.

Pippa didn't notice, but Trix saw that

Stella, Cara and Becka were lined up on their brooms, giggling behind their hands and glancing at Pippa.

This can't be good! Trix thought. She felt it in her gut. Stella wasn't helping Pippa. Trix decided to keep an eye on her new friend.

"Hey, Pippa!" Trix called. "Why don't you fly next to me?"

"Yeah, let the two bats fly together," Cara said and set Stella and Becka giggling again.

"Follow my lead and stay close!" Lulu instructed. "Would you like the training bubble?" she whispered to Pippa.

"No, I think I'm ready to fly without it," Pippa said and tucked the paper with Stella's spell in her pocket.

"All aboard, familiars!" Lulu called, and Jinx, Rascal, Twitch, Sherlock and Tabby hopped, scuttled or flew over and perched on the bushy tails of their witches' brooms.

Trix felt as if the air were supercharged as she whispered her flying incantation.

"Ready! Steady!" Lulu shouted. Trix tightly clutched her besom. She glanced back at Jinx who gave an excited *meow*! "Blast off!"

"I'm flying!" Pippa yelled as all the girls took off into the air.

"A little faster!" Lulu called and Trix leaned forwards. She felt her broom jerk underneath her. Her hands slipped and her broom wobbled but she managed to keep it under control.

It was like floating in a pool on a hot summer day mixed with sledging down a snowy hill. Lulu was zooming ahead, her beautiful gown trailing behind her. Stella was showing off, whipping up and down and from side to side when Lulu wasn't watching. Becka and Cara were laughing as they glided along. Even Pippa looked like she was having a little fun.

"Carefully angle your broom handle up," Lulu told them as she flew in a broad circle above. "That's it!" she said as they climbed higher and higher.

Trix wiggled her feet in the air. *Such a strange sensation!* They were flying over

Little Witching now. She could see her school and the run-down house on Witching Hill that she knew was secretly the headquarters of the Sisterhood of Magic. There was her house. From this high up, it looked like a doll's house. She thought she could see a tiny Aunt Belle sunning herself in the back garden. She swooped lower and waved, even though she knew Aunt Belle couldn't see her. Lulu had explained that witches were invisible to non-witches while flying.

Trix gasped when Aunt Belle smiled. She seemed to be looking right at her, but that was impossible.

"Help!" It was Pippa. "Oh, help me, please!" she cried. Pippa's broom lurched to the left and then to the right.

Trix raced ahead to get Lulu. As she did so, she noticed that Stella was staring at Pippa and flicking her finger in time with Pippa's crazy broom movements. She remembered how Stella had shared her incantation with Pippa, and guessed that somehow it enabled Stella to control Pippa's broom. Trix glared at Stella in an *I-know-what-you're-doing* way. Stella glared back in an *I-don't-care* way.

"Lulu!" Trix called. "Lulu, Pippa's in trouble!"

"Girls, go back to the airfield!" Lulu called, racing to Pippa's side. "I'll help Pippa."

As they circled to land, Trix heard Pippa scream again. *Creeping cats!* Pippa had let go of her besom. Broom, witch and familiar were tumbling through the air.

Stella looked anxious. "I just gave her a little wobble," she told Trix. "Why did she let go of her broom?"

Trix was too worried about her friend to respond to Stella.

"Pillow presto!" Lulu shouted and pointed at the hard ground coming up fast beneath Pippa and Twitch. A pillow the size of a feather bed magically appeared beneath her. Pippa bounced onto the pillow instead of splatting on the hard ground.

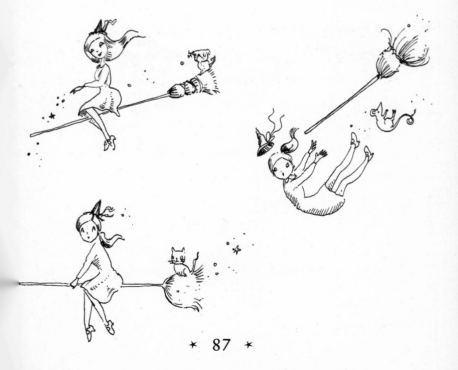

Trix raced over and helped Pippa and Twitch off the pillow. Pippa's broom was in bits. "Maybe I should give up," Pippa said. Her eyes were welling with tears.

"I think that's enough for one day." Lulu waved her arm and Stella, Becka, Cara and their familiars disappeared. "I've sent them back to school." She wrapped her arms around Trix and Pippa. "Trix, maybe you could help Pippa rebuild her broom and polish her incantation?" Trix nodded. "Pippa, you must be original," Lulu went on. "You can't copy other people's besom designs or spells." Pippa nodded. "Come in early tomorrow and I'll give you another extra lesson. We've got three days to practise. I know we can get you flying!" And with that Lulu whisked them back to the magic classroom.

Chapter Eleven

C rash landing!

That's what it felt like when Trix saw Aunt Belle's fuchsia luggage lined up in the lounge. Trix and Holly had run all the way home after school. Trix didn't want to waste a minute with her Aunt Belle.

"I'm sorry," Holly said and sank down next to Trix on the sofa. Jinx snuggled up to Trix as if he were sorry too. "Maybe it's not what you think."

But the raised voices from upstairs meant Trix was right. Aunt Belle was leaving. Trix tried not to listen. She'd learned her lesson last night, but Mum and Aunt Belle were making it difficult not to hear every word they were shouting.

"This is so typical!" Mum yelled. "Only thinking of yourself. Trix and Oscar were looking forward to spending time with you."

"What am I supposed to do?" Aunt Belle asked, her voice quieter than Mum's. "I've got a job. I have to go when they call me."

"And what job is it this time?" Mum asked. Trix couldn't believe Mum was being so mean, but she understood. She must be as disappointed as Trix was, and sometimes feeling sad made you act mad.

"I wish you could understand," Aunt Belle said. Trix could hear the creak as her parents' bedroom door opened. "I'll see you soon, Abby."

"Yes, fine. We'll wait around for you!"
Mum said and slammed the door.

The house seemed too quiet all of a
sudden. Then Trix heard Aunt Belle coming
downstairs.

"You can't leave," Trix said, rushing to
hug her aunt the moment she appeared in
the lounge. "You just got here." Aunt Belle
wore a feather-trimmed shawl around her
shoulders, and a fringe-covered handbag
swung at her hip.

"I'll be back in a few days," Aunt Belle
said, opening up her hug to let Holly in too.
"This weekend we'll do whatever you want
to do. A trip to the seaside? Shopping? You
name it!"

"OK," Trix said, even though it wasn't.
There was no point in both of them feeling
miserable. "Where are you going?"

"I've got a job booked in Edinburgh and
then one in London, but I'll be back by the
weekend." She hugged Trix and Holly tighter.
"I promise."

Aunt Belle never ever went back on a

promise to Trix. If she said she'd see her on her birthday, she did. Sometimes she didn't arrive until after ten o'clock at night, but that was still technically Trix's birthday. When she promised to send Trix and Oscar presents from every place she travelled, she did – even though it sometimes took six months for the gifts to get home and by then the sweets were stale. Trix knew Aunt Belle always tried her best.

Trix and Holly waved from the front garden until Aunt Belle's taxi had disappeared down the road.

"I need chocolate!" Trix declared and headed for the kitchen. Chocolate was one of Trix's favourite things. It sometimes made her feel a tiny bit better when bad things happened.

"I agree!" Mum said as she marched into the kitchen in her dressing gown. She'd taken the day off work to spend it with her sister and they had planned to stay in their pyjamas all day and watch their favourite films. "Let's try this!" Mum pulled a big chocolate bar from her not-so-secret-hiding place over the fridge. "Aunt Belle brought it – chilli and chocolate."

Trix and Holly's faces looked as though Mum had turned into a vampire bunny. The idea of chocolate mixed with chillies was scary silly.

"Don't knock it until you've tried it," Mum said and broke the chocolate bar into three equal pieces. "Your aunt may not be reliable, but she does bring back some strange and tasty treats."

Trix took a bite. As she chewed, all she could taste was creamy, smooth, yummy chocolate. Then her taste buds tingled as the chilli kicked in. "Creeping cats! That's amazing. You've got to try it!" Trix told Holly, who was pinching the chocolate bar between her fingers and holding it at arm's length as if it were a stinky sock covered in cobwebs.

Holly took a tiny bite. "This is good!" she agreed.

"I'm sorry Aunt Belle let you down," Mum said to Trix. "Even when she was a kid she was always sneaking away."

"But she always comes back," Trix said and gave her mum a hug. "Don't be mad at Aunt Belle. She's one of those special people who make everything better when they're around. I think that's why we miss her so much when she leaves."

"Yeah, Mrs Morgan," Holly said. She reached up beside Mum's face and appeared to pull a coin from behind her ear. "Aunt Belle's like a magic trick. She magically appears!" Holly waved her hands together and when she uncurled her fingers, the coin had vanished. "And disappears!"

"Holly, you are getting very good at your magic tricks," Mum said. Holly beamed. "You're both right. Aunt Belle *is* magical! I guess we always need to look for the best in people."

Oscar opened the back door with a bang. He was covered in mud and carrying another jar of bugs. "I'll take that!" He snatched the last bit of chocolate out of Trix's hand. As he set the jar on the counter, he knocked it over and the once-trapped army of insects now creeped, crawled and buzzed out.

"Oh, Oscar!" Mum moaned.

"Not sure I can find the best in Oscar," Trix whispered to Holly.

"We might need a microscope for *that*," Holly agreed.

Chapter Twelve

Trix's cat clock meowed eleven times.

"Wake up," Trix whispered in Jinx's ear and wiggled and stretched in her bed. The Morgan house was quiet except for the sounds of Oscar snoring in the next room.

Jinx sprang to his feet. He'd hardly slept at all. It was Friday and time for his first midnight flight.

"Where do you think we're going?" Trix asked

and studied the postcards that lined her bedroom mirror. Aunt Belle had sent them from all over the globe. "Rome? America? The North Pole?"

Jinx shook his head. Surely they wouldn't go that far. But you never knew with Lulu.

"Are you ready?" Trix asked as she finished getting dressed.

Jinx nodded. His tail flicked straight up and his fur was puffed out, making him a bouncing black and white ball of fluff. He jumped around

Trix's room, sparkling and purring.

Lulu had given her witches a special spell to recite. It was advanced magic and Jinx thought it sounded like nonsensical words, but she'd said the spell would make sure that no one discovered her witches-in-training were missing until sunrise.

Jinx shut his eyes and tried to calm his jingling, jangling excitement as Trix recited the spell. A burst of cool air ruffled his fur and then Jinx felt the tingling buzz of being magically transported. When he opened his eyes, Trix's darkened room had been replaced by the glow of the moon and the twinkle of a million stars. Lulu stood in the airfield where they had been practising all week. She'd lined up the witches' five brooms and was inspecting each one.

Jinx leaped from Trix's arm to greet Rascal, Tabby and Sherlock. Rascal was a bit nervous. His normally curly tailed drooped. Jinx knew that dogs weren't as comfortable with flying as cats. Jinx playfully nudged Rascal to tell him that everything would be all right. Sherlock showed off, soaring and diving overhead. He hooted with excitement.

"Oh, sorry I'm late," Pippa said as she and Twitch materialised in the middle of the field. "I didn't know what to wear!"

"You look great," Trix said and she was right. Pippa was wearing a long, pink flowing dress with a matching bow for her high ponytail. Jinx saw Trix look down at her own polka-dot blue jeans and the electric-green knit top Aunt Belle had bought her in Paris. He particularly liked the long necklace that had charms on it from everywhere Aunt Belle had visited. It made a beautiful tinkling sound like tiny wind chimes whenever Trix moved. The girls were wearing their tiny, pointy witch's hats. Jinx couldn't wait until they zoomed to their secret destination.

"This is the magical moment!" Lulu sing-songed. She spun around and her lacy gown shimmered in the moonlight. "Witches and familiars, to your brooms!"

"You're not going to fly on that thing, are you?" Stella asked as she pointed to Pippa's unusual flying stick. Jinx didn't think it looked much like a broom any more. Secretly Trix had helped Pippa make her very own super-unique besom. They had tied bunches of twigs up and down the handle – the way Pippa had designed her broom at their very first flying lesson.

"You haven't seen her fly on it," Trix stepped up beside Pippa. Jinx loved that Trix always stood up for her friends. "Stay close to me," Trix whispered to Pippa.

"Everyone ready?" Lulu said as she and Sparkles mounted her broom at the front of the pack. "Now recite your magical flying incantations." Whispered spells filled the night and tickled Jinx's ears. The air felt electric with magic. "It's time to fly," Lulu said and floated into the air. "Follow me."

Jinx dug his claws into the broom. He felt the rush as they took flight. Pippa flew close by Trix's side as the other girls raced ahead.

"Go ahead," Trix told Pippa. Jinx knew Pippa had been practising a special routine. Pippa's unique broom design allowed her to fly as gracefully backwards and sideways as she did forwards.

"Do you think I should?" Pippa asked, sounding a bit unsure.

"Absolutely!" Trix said, giving Pippa a smile. Pippa zoomed forwards, skidding left and then right, but never losing her balance or control of her besom. She spiralled through the air, twirling Twitch and her broom around and around. Upside down. Right-side up. Right-side down. Jinx's tummy was doing loopity-loops just watching.

"Look at her go!" Trix said in a way that Jinx thought sounded like a proud mother cat.

"How did you do that?"

"Can you teach me?"

"Wow! That's great!" Stella, Cara and Becka called to Pippa.

Now Pippa led the pack and the girls followed every swirl of her broom.

Trix called to Pippa but she didn't seem to hear her. The other girls were laughing and trying to copy Pippa's flying tricks. Trix slumped on her broom.

"Do you think this means Pippa's not my friend any more?" Trix asked Jinx.

Jinx shook his head as though he had wet ears. But Trix didn't notice. She was too busy watching the other girls having fun without her.

Jinx glanced down. His yellow eyes opened as

wide as they could go. Through a break in the clouds Jinx could see the sparkling lights of a city. It looked like a glittery jewellery box from this high up. He meowed to get Trix's attention and then pointed a paw as the huge face of a clock came into focus.

"There's Big Ben, the Houses of Parliament and the London Eye!" Trix exclaimed, flying closer and closer to the lights and farther and farther away from Lulu and the other witches.

As they dipped into a cloud, the air cooled and Jinx's fur felt damp. Meow! The clouds weren't soft and fluffy like he'd expected they would be. They were cold and wet. The clouds seemed to roll in and surround them. MEOW! Jinx cried again.

"Creeping cats! I can't see!" Trix cried. Jinx dug his claws into the wood of the broom. His whiskers and ears flattened and his fur stopped sparkling. They were well and truly lost.

Chapter Thirteen

Trix had never felt more lost and alone in her life. She didn't know which way she'd come from or which way she was going. She couldn't see anything. Mist coated her curls and made everything droop. Jinx crept up behind her so she could feel his warm body pressed against hers.

"Thanks, Jinx," she said and reached around to stroke him.

She heard a distant buzzing which was becoming a roar. *An aeroplane!* She started to descend. She didn't want a mid-air collision and planes always flew very high in the sky. But then she remembered her quick peek of London – all those tall buildings. She didn't want to fly so low that she crashed into Big Ben. She slowed her broom so she was hovering in space. She started to tremble. Lulu and the others would have to realise she was missing. They'd come looking for her soon.

But then Trix remembered how Pippa had deserted her for Becka and the Enchanted Grove girls just when she'd thought they'd become friends.

Trix was getting cold. Her teeth were starting to chatter and words were getting jumbled in her brain.

The roaring was getting louder by the second. She pressed herself flat against her broomstick. She knew witches were invisible when they flew. Even if she weren't hidden in a cloud, the aeroplane pilot wouldn't see her.

Roar!

The plane zoomed above her and a gust of wind bounced her from side to side, but the plane had cleared a path through the clouds.

"Trix! Trix! Where are you?" Pippa was calling her.

"I'm right here!" Trix yelled. The back of her broom began to glow. It was Jinx! His fur was sparkling. Her familiar was like a beacon, showing Pippa the way!

And suddenly Pippa burst through the clouds, her pink gown and Twitch's lavender fur reflecting the lights of London as they raced to the rescue.

"I found her! She's over here!" Pippa yelled to the others.

"I've never been more happy to see anyone in my life," Trix said as Pippa flew to her side. "You saved me!"

"You saved me first," Pippa said with a laugh. "I wouldn't be flying if you and Lulu hadn't helped me."

"Magic marbles! You scared me," Lulu

said. "Well done, Pippa, for finding her."
Lulu glanced at Big Ben. "Is that the time?
We've got to hurry. Your mentors will be
arriving soon."

"Where are we going?" Stella asked, pulling
up on the other side of Trix.

"All in good time, my lovelies," Lulu said
with a smile and Trix felt the scary feelings
from before fade away. Lulu beckoned the
girls forwards.

"I'll look after Trix," Stella called to Lulu.
Then she turned her pinched face to Trix.
"Try not to ruin everything, Trixibelle." She
sounded so snotty. Trix hated the way Stella
made her feel even colder and more alone
than she had when she was lost in the cloud.
Stella didn't wait for Trix. She zoomed off
after Lulu, followed closely by Becka and
Cara. "Come on, Pippa," Stella called and
waved Pippa over. "Don't you want to ride
with your friends?"

Pippa looked at Trix and then at Stella. She
glided closer to Trix – so close that she could
reach out and hold Trix's hand. "I *am* flying

with my friend," she said. And they flew
hand in hand over the sparkling streets of
London.

Chapter Fourteen

T rix and Pippa followed Lulu as she zipped over the city.

"Oh, I think that's Hype Park!" Pippa pointed and pulled away from Trix.

"It's called Hyde Park," Trix laughed.

"Watch closely!" Lulu said and recited an advanced magic spell.

Below her, Trix could see Hyde Park's pathways, fields, trees and the lake she knew was called the Serpentine. But then the scene suddenly changed. Trix blinked and blinked again. She couldn't believe her eyes. A whole new garden had appeared in the middle of the park.

They landed in a rose-ringed patch of grass. The flowers glowed with a ruby light. The air was perfumed by the blooming roses and a chorus of birds sang a sweet song. The surrounding trees seemed to dance in the night air.

"Welcome to the Enchanted Garden!" Lulu said, spinning with her arms outstretched. The air seemed to respond and began to swirl, showering the girls and their familiars with petals.

"Only those of us in the Sisterhood of Magic can come to the Enchanted Garden," Lulu explained. "This place was created by Cinderella's fairy godmother. Fairy godmothers travel the globe granting magical wishes to girls and boys. She wanted to give us a special place where we could gather."

"Does everyone have a fairy godmother?" Trix asked, thinking of the many wishes she'd made – some of which had come true and some of which had remained locked inside her heart.

Lulu picked up a petal-covered Jinx and handed him to Trix. "Yes, everyone has a fairy godmother, but most people never know it."

Trix hugged Jinx close. He was definitely a wish come true.

"Why don't people know it?" Stella asked. "Shouldn't fairy godmothers get credit for their work?"

"Some people call it luck or coincidence when their wishes come true," Lulu said, smoothing Stella's hair. "Others think their wishes are granted through hard work and determination." She walked over and hugged Pippa in one arm and Cara in the other. "Work and determination always help, but secretly many, many good things are granted with a little *extra* help from fairy godmothers."

Trix tried to let Lulu's words sink in. These were very big thoughts and Trix knew it might take a long time for her to understand.

"Every young witch needs a guide on her path to becoming a fairy godmother," Lulu continued. She gathered the girls together. "Tonight I will introduce you to your mentors. Like your familiar, this person will be with you through thick and thin, through light and shadow, for question and answer."

Lulu raised her hands to the sky. Four bright stars seemed to twinkle overhead. "Allow me to introduce to you . . ." The stars grew brighter and brighter as Lulu spoke. "Regina!"

REGINA

A tall, thin, beautiful redhead swooped from the sky. She landed next to Pippa. Trix was sure she'd seen her on TV before, but she couldn't remember when or where.

"Camilla and Desiree!" Lulu announced, and women who could have been twins parked their brooms beside Cara and Becka.

CAMILLA   DESIREE

"And welcome Bess!" Lulu said as a short pudgy woman with grey hair rolled in curlers

BESS

and wearing a red silk dressing-gown slowly sailed down next to Stella.

"Grandmama!" Stella exclaimed as the old lady kissed Stella on both cheeks.

"Surprise!" Bess said, striking a silly super-model pose. "I begged Lulu to let me mentor you. We'll have such fun. I can't believe my little Stella-wella Bear is a witchy-poo already."

Stella cringed. She looked surprised but not pleased.

"And finally . . ." Lulu looked heavenward. "Last but not least . . . Late but not forgotten

. . ." She searched the starry sky. "Oh, I'm sure she's coming! Perhaps she got delayed at Gatwick airport. That happens sometimes."

Lulu put an arm around Trix and Jinx and whispered, "She's the perfect mentor for you. I was *her* mentor when she was your age and you remind me of her. You have the same sparkle and natural ability to help others." Lulu's face twisted with worry but then she forced a smile. "Never mind. She'll be here when she gets here." Lulu kissed Trix on the top of her head and moved to the centre of the Enchanted Garden. "Tonight, fly with your mentors. Get to know each other, and—"

"But I already know my grandmama," Stella interrupted.

"Don't be rude, dear," Stella's Grandmama Bess corrected. "Let Lulu finish. Continue, Lulu darling!" Bess said with a posh accent that didn't match her curler-filled hair and – Trix noticed – bare feet.

"You know Bess as your grandmama,

but now you will get to know her as the masterful fairy godmother she is!" Lulu told Stella. She smiled at each pair. "Have a wonderful flight and a magical night. The girls must be home before sunrise."

The ribbons on Trix's pointy hat fluttered as witches and mentors took flight. It was the most magical thing she'd ever seen as their besoms created a rainbow arch of light and they disappeared into the night sky. She only wished she could be a part of it.

Chapter Fifteen

Suddenly a gust of wind rushed through the trees setting them swaying and sending petals dancing in the air. Jinx hopped, skipped and scampered, chasing the petals this way and that. Trix scanned the sky for any sign of her mentor. Maybe her mentor had had second thoughts. Trix wasn't the best witch of the batch, was she? Or maybe she'd got lost. Trix knew how easy it was to get distracted with so many lights in London.

"Perhaps I should go home," Trix told Lulu as the bells of Big Ben rang out over a sleepy London.

"There!" Lulu pointed to a pink dot that grew in intensity before shooting like a star across the night sky. "She knows how to make an entrance!"

As the light drew closer, the silhouette of a spiky-haired witch came into focus. Her besom was crooked with tassels swishing underneath, and perched on the back of the broom was what looked like a big-eared bear cub. But as the witch drew nearer, her familiar came into focus and Trix realised it was a koala.

The witched waved to Trix and Jinx and her broom zigzagged through the sky leaving a trail of pink smoke behind her.

She's writing something in the sky! Trix realised, and watched as the letters looped together.

She couldn't believe it. Her name was

Trixibelle

written in pink high above London for the
world to see. She wished Holly or Pippa
could share this moment with her.

"Are you surprised?" Lulu asked, a smile
lighting up her face.

"Um, yes, the sky writing is amazing," Trix
replied. "But who is it?"

"Trixibelle," Lulu said.

Trix looked confused.

"Trixibelle Spellwright," Lulu repeated –
and finally Trix understood.

"Aunt Belle," Trix breathed, and then,
"Aunt Belle!" she called to her mentor who
was also her aunt. She couldn't believe it. Her
aunt was a witch and a fairy godmother! So
many things made sense now – how Aunt

Belle had made salty fairy cakes taste sweet, and how she'd sent Trix the perfect present with a good-luck message about flying.

Aunt Belle swooped down and wrapped Trix in a tight hug. "I've wanted to tell you so many times," she said.

"When you flew off to those places, you were really granting wishes," Trix realised.

Aunt Belle nodded.

"Is Mum a witch?" Trix asked, feeling funny that maybe her mum had been keeping secrets from her too.

"Your mum is magical but she's not a witch," Aunt Belle said. "I mean, your mum makes magic the old-fashioned way like all non-witches can – by being kind and fun and a great person! But there's a long line of fairy godmothers in our family: Great-aunt Sadie, Cousin Amy, your Great-great-grandmother Frieda."

"You two had better get going," Lulu said. She gave Aunt Belle a hug.

"Let's show 'em how Trixibelles fly!" Aunt Belle said, mounting her besom and giving her familiar a scratch behind the ear. "This is Aussie, my familiar."

Jinx raced over to inspect Aussie. "This is Jinx," Trix told her aunt.

"I think I almost stepped on you at the airport," Aunt Belle said, giving Jinx a stroke. "It's been hard not laughing at your tricks."

"All this time you could see him too!" Trix exclaimed.

"And now we can share all kinds of secrets," Aunt Belle said. "And we'll start with the best flying tour of London ever." Aunt Belle zipped off into the night.

Jinx jumped onto Trix's broom, Trix whispered her flying incantation and then they zoomed after Aunt Belle.

"What's the best part of being a fairy godmother?" Trix asked as they wove between the pods of the London Eye.

Aunt Belle hovered at the top of the great wheel and looked out over the Houses of Parliament and down the Thames to St Paul's. "This is pretty amazing right now,"

Aunt Belle said. "But helping people is even better."

"And what's the worst part?" Trix asked, but she thought she already knew the answer.

"Keeping secrets can be fun, but it's difficult too," Aunt Belle said and headed for Big Ben.

Trix followed. "Mum couldn't ever be mad at you if she knew what you really did."

"Your mum would think I was crazy if I told her," Aunt Belle sighed. She playfully brushed the hands of Big Ben. "But it's better now that you know. Being a fairy godmother is a privilege and a huge responsibility. Believe me when I say that you were born to do this." She winked at Trix. "But that's enough learning for tonight. We can talk when we're on the ground. Now – let's *fly!*"

Trix agreed. Her head was buzzing with a squillion questions, but for now she just wanted to enjoy this magical night with her magical aunt.

They peeked in through a window at Buckingham Palace and played hide and seek in the turrets of the Tower of London. Trix chased Aunt Belle down the Thames. And then they raced the sunrise back home.

Two uniquely magical witches, sharing secrets.

Don't miss the next exciting adventure
in the *Magic Trix* series

Birthday Wishes

Available May 2013!
Read on for a special preview of the first
chapter.

Chapter One

"Slobber from a spotless Dalmatian?" Lulu asked her witches-in-training. She held up a glass jar filled with a cloudy thick liquid.

Trix's brain felt gooey, as if Lulu's lesson on magical mixtures had somehow turned her mind into a treacle sponge soaked in custard. Trix had recently turned ten years old and discovered she had the gift of magic. Every week day, she and four other new witches

took lessons from Lulu on how to
use their magical powers.

*What potion would use dog
slobber?*

"It's a key ingredient
for many stain-
removing potions,"
Stella piped up. She
smiled a horribly smug
smile. She was right
and she knew it. There
was nothing wrong with
right answers, but Stella
made her rightness seem oh so wrong.

"That is correct!" Lulu exclaimed and
returned the jar with its sloshing contents to
the bookcase. Lulu picked up what appeared
to be an empty jar. "Does anyone remember
what this is?"

Trix hoped that wasn't the stink of a skunk.
Lulu had opened the burp of a walrus at the
beginning of the lesson and the fishy smell
still lingered in the magic classroom.

"Eerie silence from outer space," Pippa

answered with a satisfied swish of her high ponytail.

Trix raised her eyebrows in surprise. When had Pippa become a genius at potions? "Well done," Trix echoed Lulu's praise of her friend.

Over the past week, Lulu had taught them about the weird and wonderful ingredients stored in the magic classroom's huge bookcase. Lulu was responsible for training the newest witches in the Sisterhood of Magic in the hope that they would become fairy godmothers one day.

Today Lulu had surprised them with a quiz. The girls sat facing her, raising their hands when they knew the answer. Each witch had a magical familiar as a companion. All the familiars sat quietly on their witches' laps – except Trix's familiar. Jinx – her cheeky black and white kitten – scampered about the room as if dancing some strange cat jig to imaginary music.

Lulu asked question after question. After a little thought, Cara knew the recipe for the classic laughing potion. Then Lulu asked

Becka's familiar, Sherlock the owl, to point his wing to each ingredient on the top shelf, and Becka guessed every single item correctly.

"Trix, which potion requires water off a duck's back and a tornado swirl?" Lulu held up a jar with a grey funnel cloud inside. The jar vibrated in her hands. "And it must be mixed with the tears of a tiger at the stroke of midnight."

Creeping cats! Potions were too much like science experiments. Mr Beaker had made Trix sit at the back of the class whenever he was performing an experiment. She had melted his glasses once, and ever since he'd declared her a safety hazard when it came to science.

Trix begged her brain to be smarter.

"Come on, Trix," Stella moaned. "This is an easy one."

Oooooh, Stella made her so mad! She was embarrassing Trix in front of Lulu and the other witches. Trix didn't know the right answer but, even so, Stella's behaviour was unforgivable.

Wait! That's it!

"That's the recipe for a forgiveness potion!"
Trix exclaimed, smiling. Jinx leaped onto
Trix's lap. His spots sparkled like they always
did when he was proud of Trix.

"Magically marvellous!" Lulu spun in
a circle setting the lacy hem of her gown
swishing at her ankles and the bracelets on
her wrists jingle-jangling. "Now let's review
a few of the spells that must accompany

certain potions," Lulu said when she stopped spinning. She lifted the biggest book off the bookcase and plonked it on a nearby table.

Lulu continued her lesson but her words seemed to float like clouds over Trix's head. It was hard to concentrate when Trix had a super-duper secret – tomorrow she was throwing her best friend Holly a surprise party.

She usually hated keeping secrets. She told Holly everything – well, everything except the fact that she was a witch. Now, Holly was turning ten and Trix was sure – OK, she wasn't one hundred per cent certain, but she did hope, pray and wish with every cell in her body and every spark in her brain – that Holly would discover she was a witch too, just like Trix had on the night of her tenth birthday.

Trix's body felt like a shaken fizzy drink ready to explode. She shivered off her excitement and tried to concentrate on Lulu's lesson.

"What's that?" Pippa pointed to a bowl

half-full of white cubes made of teeny tiny crystals that reflected the green glow of Lulu's cauldron. Pippa's familiar, Twitch, a lavender rat, scuttled over and sniffed the white substance.

"Oh, that." Lulu plopped one of the cubes in her mouth.

Trix's eyes narrowed and she gagged a little as she imagined the awful possibilities. Was that the dandruff from a meerkat? Ash from an erupting volcano? Freeze-dried dragon scales?

Lulu laughed when she spotted the pained expression on Trix's face. "They're sugar lumps for my tea." Lulu placed the sugar bowl on the shelf by her rainbow-striped teapot. "I can see your brains are overflowing with witch-tastic knowledge," Lulu said, straightening the rows and rows of jars. "And that's enough for this magically magnificent lesson. Have wonderful weekends, my dears!"

As Trix turned to go, something terrible happened in what felt like painfully slow

motion. Her brain screamed that it couldn't
be real, but her eyes showed that it definitely
and dreadfully was . . .

Stella elbowed past Trix, which caused her
to slip on a drop of rainbow essence Lulu had
spilled earlier. As she went crashing to the
floor, Trix knocked the bookcase. It wobbled
and the glass jars clinked on the shelves.
For a moment, the bookcase and its magical
contents seemed to hover in the precarious
place between tipping and falling.

Trix, squeezed her eyes shut, covered her
head and wondered if she was about to be
squashed!

the orion star

Sign up for **the orion star**
newsletter to get inside information
about your favourite children's authors
as well as exclusive competitions and
early reading copy giveaways.

www.orionbooks.co.uk/newsletters

Follow  on **twitter**

Orion
Children's Books